THIS CANDLEWICK BOOK BELONGS TO:

Thanks, Amy
A. H.

For my mother, Irene,
who always thought everything
I drew was just great
S. W. S.

Text copyright © 1996 by Amy Hest
Illustrations copyright © 1996 by Sheila White Samton

First paperback edition 1997

The Library of Congress has cataloged the hardcover edition as follows:

Hest, Amy.
Jamaica Louise James / Amy Hest ; illustrated by Sheila White Samton. – 1st ed.
Summary: On her eighth birthday Jamaica receives paints which she uses to
surprise her grandmother and to brighten the subway station where Grammy works.
ISBN 978-1-56402-348-3 (hardcover)
[1. Painting – Fiction. 2. Birthdays – Fiction. 3. Afro-Americans – Fiction.]
I. Samton, Sheila White, ill. II. Title.
PZ7.H4375Jam 1996
[E] – dc20   95-20581

ISBN 978-0-7636-0284-0 (paperback)

11 12 13 14 15 16 SWT 23 22 21 20 19 18 17 16 15 14

Printed in Dongguan, Guangdong, China

This book was typeset in Cafeteria.
The illustrations were done in acrylic, gouache, and watercolor.

Candlewick Press
99 Dover Street
Somerville, Massachusetts 02144

visit us at www.candlewick.com

JAMAICA LOUISE JAMES

Amy Hest

illustrated by

Sheila White Samton

CANDLEWICK PRESS

I was the one with the COOL idea...

It happened last winter and the mayor put my name on a golden plaque. It's down in the subway station at 86th and Main. You can see it if you go there.

That's me. You better believe it!
Want to hear my big idea?

I'll tell but you've got to listen to the whole story, not just a part of it. Mama says my stories go on . . . and on . . . Whenever I'm just at the beginning of one, she tells me, "Get to the point, Jamaica!" or "Snap to it, baby!" But I like lacing up the details, this way and that.

This story begins with me. I have a big artist pad with one hundred big pages and five colored pencils with perfect skinny points. Sometimes I set myself up on the top step of our building, where everyone can see me. Everything I see is something I want to draw.

At night, Mama and Grammy and I cuddle on the couch while the city quiets down. I show them every picture every night. Sometimes I tell a story as I go. Sometimes they ask a question like, Why does the man's coat have triangle pockets? Other times we don't say a word.

Now look at me on birthday #8. Grammy and Mama dance around my bed. "Open your present!" they shout. "We can't wait another minute!"

Know what they did? They bought me a real paint set—with eight little tubes of color and two paint brushes. Paint sets cost a lot, I worry. "My! My!" they say. "Are you going to spend birthday #8 WORRYING, when you can be doing something wonderful such as PAINTING THE WORLD?"

So that's when I get my BIG idea.

Now, this part of the story tells about my grammy,
who leaves for work when it is still dark. Sometimes
I wake up halfway when she slides out of bed. In
winter she gets all layered, starting with the
long-underwear layer.

She and Mama whisper in the kitchen. They drink
that strong black coffee. Grammy scoops up her
brown lunch bag and goes outside.

I'm scared in the night. Not Grammy. At 86th and
Main she goes down . . . and down . . . into the
subway station.

All day long people line up at Grammy's token booth.
They give her a dollar or four quarters, and she slides
a token into their hand. Then they rush off to catch
the train.

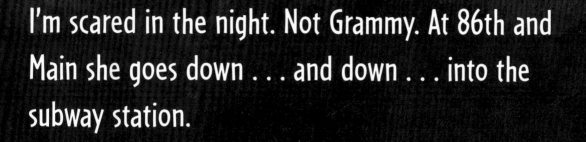

Subway

Now, I like subways because the seats are hot pink and because they go very fast. But I don't like subway stations. Especially the one at 86th and Main. There are too many steep steps (fifty-six) and too many grownups who all look mad. The walls are old tile walls without any color.

When Grammy comes home, she sews and talks about the people she sees, like Green-Hat Lady or Gentleman with the Red Bow Tie. Mama reads and hums. But I paint, blending all those colors until they look just right. Every day I add a picture to my collection and every day I think about my cool idea.

At last it's the morning of Grammy's birthday. Mama and I get up early. We get all layered and sneak outside. Mama holds my hand. I am scared but also VERY EXCITED. We swoosh along in our boots in the dark in the snow. At 86th and Main we go down . . .

and down . . .

fifty-six steep steps.

31 11

We don't buy a token at the token booth. We don't take
a ride on the subway. What we do is hang a painting on the
old tile wall. Then another. And another . . . and one more.
Before you know it, that station is all filled up with color.

Surprise!

we shout when Grammy comes clomping down the steps. She looks all around that station. "Jamaica Louise James," she calls, "come right here so I can give you a big hug, baby!"

So now you know the whole story. Everyone sure is in love with my subway station! You'd be surprised. People are talking to each other—some even smile. "That looks like me!" says a lady in a green hat to a gentleman with a red bow tie. Then Grammy tells everyone about Jamaica Louise James, age 8.

THAT'S ME. YOU BETTER BELIEVE IT!